Hanako Masutani

# Emi
## and
# Mini

illustrations by
Stéphane Jorisch

**TRADEWIND BOOKS**
Vancouver · London

# CHAPTER 1

**M**y name is Emiko. But you can call me Emi. Nicknames are my favourite.

I also like polka dots. And green. I like curly noodles and curly fries and bacon fried rice with *umeboshi*. I like playing soccer, especially goalie, and I like to draw. Most of all, I like dogs.

My mom and I just moved to a small apartment in a big city. We have lots of pretty plants and fat books and colourful rice bowls that stack. I also have the world's best cousins, Soren and Mei. But they live back in Comox, a town on Vancouver Island. That's where we moved from.

Every day my cousins text me silly photos with their tongues sticking out to say they miss me. I text the same kind of goofy photos back. Some days, Soren and Mei also send photos of Hugo, their huge Bernese mountain dog. Hugo is never too busy to let me use him as a pillow. He's shaggy and slobbery, roly-poly and soft-eyed.

Our landlady says we can't have a dog. Our apartment is too small. But if I could have a dog, I'd name her Frida. I'd let her sleep under my covers. I'd take her for walks in all kinds of weather. If I had a dog, I would never feel lonely.

# CHAPTER 2

**M**y birthday is just around the corner. On the weekend, Mom and I plan it at the kitchen table with my papers and pencil crayons.

"I want gold balloons." I draw them. "And red streamers." I squiggle them all over the page. "The red is for Mei, of course." We both know that red is Mei's favourite. "I can't wait to see them," I say.

Mom gives me a sad look.

"Emi. We're not going to be able to go and see your cousins for your birthday. We can't take the ferry again so soon after moving. It's expensive."

My heart drops down to my stomach, where hearts do not belong.

"I know it's disappointing. We'll go during spring break, okay? We'll have a party for you with your cousins then."

I nod, but my face feels hot, and my eyes start to fill up. "Sure," I say.

"Maybe you can invite someone from school or soccer."

I shake my head. I don't know anyone at school or soccer who I could invite to my party. Not yet.

"We'll talk to Soren and Mei on Zoom on your birthday. We can blow out candles and everything." Mom holds my hand between hers, making our warm "hand sandwich."

"Okay," I say. I look out the window. People are out walking their dogs in the rain. "Look, Mom." I sniff. There's a French bulldog going down the other side of the street in a shiny gold raincoat, like a walking birthday balloon.

"Posh puppy!" Mom says. We laugh. "Emiko, I know how much you love dogs." Mom plays with her hair the way that tells me she is thinking. "How about I call our landlord? Maybe I can convince her to let us have a pet."

"Really?" Suddenly my heart is breakdancing in my chest.

"Don't get too excited, Emi. She may say no."

I nod fast a whole bunch of times.

"Remember, animals need a lot of care and attention."

"Yes! Yes! Yes!"

Mom smiles and pulls out her phone.

# CHAPTER 3

**M**om wants me to have the stuff I want, especially for my birthday. I know that. When I do not get what I want, it's because there is no way my mom can help me get it or because the thing I want is not exactly good for me. Like eating all my Easter candy in one day. Or riding my bike super fast down the alley without my helmet on. So when Mom calls our landlord, I know she'll do her best to help me get a dog. Dogs are not even a little bit bad for me.

I run into my room and pour my excitement out onto my scrap paper in a rainbow of dog pictures. I draw a zillion.

Eventually Mom comes in. "There is good news and bad news," she says.

"No dog?" My heart stops dancing.

"No. But she did say we could get a pet in a cage. A bird, maybe, or a turtle . . ."

My heart curls up tight, hard and sharp.

"Emi? Are you okay?"

I shake my head. I am not okay. If I open my mouth, I will cry. Mom squeezes me, so the tears come out anyway.

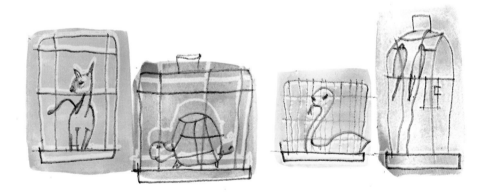

# CHAPTER 4

**W**e park outside the animal shelter on the way home from school on Friday. Mom turns in her front seat and looks at me. "Emi, try to keep an open mind."

"I know," I say. "I will." I'm lucky I can get a pet, even if it can't be a dog.

The room with the small pets is loud with animal sounds and smells kind of like a barn and kind of like a hospital. It's noisy and a bit gross. But there are stacks of cages, all full of pets—guinea pigs, bunnies, even a parrot.

I give each pet a hard look. One is eating a weed. Another rodent is running on a wheel.

Then, from right beside me, I hear an urgent squeak. I turn to see who's making the sound.

# CHAPTER 5

It's a small furry animal with big ears, maybe a rat.

The shelter worker comes up to me. "You like her?"

"Maybe," I say. "What is she?"

"She's a Syrian hamster, a friendly one. She's already grown up, so as you can see, she's nice and calm."

Mom comes over and we watch the woman bring the hamster out of her cage. "Wow," Mom says. "She seems big for a hamster."

The shelter worker nods. "She's the biggest one I've ever seen."

I look at the hamster. They might think she's big, but she's little. Like a puppy.

# CHAPTER 6

It's fun to get new things, especially when they are early birthday presents. I put my new hamster cage in the corner of my room. I put a new hamster dish with food into the cage and hang the new water bottle on the outside. Its spout pops inside so my hamster can drink from the bottle like a baby. Why is it that new things are so much fun?

Last, I lift my hamster out of her carrying box and into her new home. I sit back to see what she'll do. Will she eat? Drink? Will she run around in happy hamster circles?

My hamster waddles over to a corner of the cage. She curls up into a ball and goes to sleep. This pet is no puppy. A puppy would be excited about new things, just like me.

My new pet sleeps for the rest of the day. At bedtime, just as I'm snuggling deep under my duvet, I hear scuffling coming from the hamster corner. I sit up. My hamster is running around her cage, kicking up sawdust. She stops when she sees me, stands on her hind feet and chews the bars of her cage so they rattle.

I get out of bed and peek at her. "What are you up to?"

My hamster takes one look at me and heads to her food bowl as if she understands and is answering me. Her front paws look like tiny hands. She uses them to pick up corn kernels and stuff them into her cheeks. Her face bulges. I can't believe how much she can stuff in. I have to admit, it's kind of cute.

"You are a funny one," I whisper. I get back into bed and fall asleep to the sound of her busy munching.

## CHAPTER 7

"Happy Birthday!" Soren and Mei squeeze their heads into my computer screen. They sing 'Happy Birthday' so loud I have to turn the volume down.

"Thanks, you two. Also, thanks for the paints." I hold up the watercolours they sent me in the mail. "I'm going to make so many pictures with these."

I'm just about to tell them about my hamster when Soren says, "Check out what we just got." He lifts up something small and white.

I lean closer. "What IS that?"

"Our new puppy! We're naming her Joyce."

"Or Sunjammer!" Mei yells.

Soren gives his sister his annoyed look. Then he grins back at me. "Look at how creamy soft she is." He strokes the puppy, and she really does look cotton-ball soft.

I don't say that. I say, "I can't see how your dog feels, Soren. I can't feel through a screen."

"Oh yeah. I forgot." The puppy licks Soren's cheek.

"Her face is all pushed in," I say. "Kind of funny looking. I bet Hugo will be jealous."

"Hugo loves Sunjammer," says Mei. The white puppy is all over them both, licking and sniffing and nuzzling.

"I have to go," I say, even though I do not. Mei and Soren are so busy with the new puppy they don't even notice when I leave our Zoom room.

# CHAPTER 8

**M**y birthday feels long. And flat. Like a squished loaf of bread. After we eat curly fries for a late lunch and as much ice cream cake as we can without getting sick, Mom asks, "What did Soren and Mei think of your hamster?"

"I didn't have time to show them."

Mom looks confused but says, "Did you know that a hamster can learn its own name? Why don't you take your hamster out of her cage and see?"

I go back to my bedroom and take my hamster out of her cage, even though I know Mom is wrong. Hamsters cannot learn their names. Not like a puppy can.

At first, we just look at each other, me and my hamster. We're face to face on the carpet.

She squeaks like she did at the shelter.

"Come, Hammy, Hammy," I try. My hamster does not budge a muscle.

Okay, maybe she can learn to sit. "Sit," I say. She does not.

I carry her to the couch in the living room.

"What are you going to call her?" Mom asks from the kitchen.

"Don't know," I say. "Hammy?"

"Really?" Mom walks over and sits down beside us. She puts a bowl of popcorn down on the coffee table. "Maybe you both need a treat. I hear a little bit of popcorn is safe for hamsters."

I sit my hamster on my lap. Maybe she will curl up like a puppy and nibble on her snack. But no. My hamster scampers down my leg like it's a ladder and rolls onto the carpet.

I glare at Mom. "She's not friendly," I say. "See! I need a real puppy like Soren and Mei!"

"Watch out!" says Mom.

My hamster is running away.

**M**y hamster speeds across the floor. I pull a blanket off the couch to try and net her with it, but she is way too fast. In under one second, my new pet is gone.

Can a hamster vanish? Mom and I look everywhere. We look under the couch and under the chairs and crawl on our hands and knees everywhere we think a hamster might fit. Our place is small for humans but, for hamster hiding spots, it is enormous.

This is my fault. I should have given her a

name. Maybe if I did, I would be able to call her now, and she would come running.

Mom and I make curly noodles in cream sauce for my birthday dinner, but I don't eat much. Where would a hamster hide? I look under the couch and chairs again. I think I see something, but it's just a sock. When Mom tells me I have to go to bed, I check the cage. There's no hamster in it. I snuggle under my duvet and feel sad. My hamster likes to snuggle in her toilet paper nests. I miss her scuffling sound and the way she stuffs her cheeks.

# CHAPTER 11

"Did you know a wild hamster can run five miles in one night?" Mom looks up from the Google search on her phone. We're eating bacon fried rice for breakfast. Mom knows my favourites.

"There are wild hamsters?" I try to imagine my hamster living in the wild, hopping over dirt and scurrying through tall grasses, all scruffy and fierce. "That's a long way for something small to run. I bet that's more than a puppy can go in one day."

"Definitely," says Mom.

We eat without talking for a while. Even though my hamster sleeps during the day, our place feels emptier without her.

"Do you think she was trying to run away?" I ask Mom. "Is it because I didn't love her enough?"

"Well. I think she's probably curious. After all, she's never been in an apartment before. If I were her, I would want to explore. What would you do if you were her?"

"If I were her, I would hide in a small space all by myself. But then I would feel lonely."

Mom nods very slowly.

"And I might get scared."

"Scared that no one would find you?"

"Yeah. And scared of the world outside."

Mom waves me over to her lap and gives me one of her good warm hugs.

# CHAPTER 12

In the afternoon, I draw a zillion pictures of my hamster. I try to get her eyes right. They are like bright black diamonds. But then her nose is too big. And her paws. Fun fact— hamsters have four toes in front and five in the back. One by one, I hold my pictures up. A few would make good LOST HAMSTER signs. I sigh.

I search everywhere all over again.

No hamster. I sit down and look out the window. A girl my age is walking out of our building in a soccer jersey and cleats. I had no idea there was someone my age in the building who plays soccer. Maybe I'll play against her team one day. Maybe she likes hamsters.

The girl's dad comes out of our building, and I watch them walk down Main Street. The usual dogs and owners are out for their evening walk. The girl stops to pet a big bouncy dog. And I realize something surprising. I'm not looking at the dog and wishing it was mine. I just want my hamster back. She should be home, sleeping in her nest.

I get an idea.

"Emi! What are you doing?"

I've got a cozy pile of toilet paper strips on the couch. "I'm tearing up this roll to make a nest for my hamster. Maybe she'll come out to sleep in it."

Mom looks like she wants to say something about the mess on the couch, but she just sits down beside me. "Maybe she will."

We sit very quiet. Quiet like, well, hamsters. In that quiet, I hear a small sound, a scuffling sound, over by the fridge.

Mom looks at me. She hears it too. She speaks in a whisper. "Emiko, my love. I am going to stand up very quietly and sneak into the kitchen."

Mom bends down by the fridge. That is where she finds my hamster. My hamster is beside the fridge, way at the back, and covered in lint. She looks sticky and miserable. I am so relieved and still scared at the same time, my heart doesn't know how to beat.

"See if you can get her, Emi," says Mom. "Your arms are smaller and might be able to squeeze through."

I get my arm to fit between the fridge and the side of the bottom kitchen cupboard, but I can't reach far enough. My hand is not even close to my hamster. "I can't. Maybe you can reach."

Only the first half of Mom's hand can fit through the gap. Mom shakes her head. "We're going to have to think of another way."

# CHAPTER 13

**M**om makes dinner while my tummy rumbles. "My hamster must be hungry too," I say. I am still on the floor by the fridge keeping watch over her. "And thirsty. Maybe I can give her some greens?"

"I'll check the SPCA hamster guide." Mom is a pro at finding things out on the internet. "Okay. I've got it. It says they can eat a bit of egg, but not too much, or they'll get fat." My mom smiles and hands me my dinner. It's omelette, *gai lan*, and rice.

"Perfect!" I take a tiny bit of my omelette and put it on the floor between me and the fridge. My hamster looks half asleep. She doesn't seem to notice the egg. "What else can I try? What are their favourites?"

It takes a moment for Mom to type, scroll

and find the answer. "Apparently, corn, sunflower seeds and peanuts."

"Can I use some of our canned corn?"

"Of course."

I jump up, put my plate on the table, and get a can of corn out of the cupboard. But my hamster doesn't even notice the little sun-yellow pile of sweet corn I've put down for her. She ignores it like she ignored the omelette.

"You need to eat some supper too," Mom says. I get my plate and lie back down by the fridge. Maybe if she sees me eating, my hamster will feel hungry.

"Emi, I've found something. It says we can make a trap to catch your hamster while we sleep. All we need is a bucket and something to make a ramp or steps out of. Then we put treats on the ramp and your hamster will eat them one by one, all the way up to the top and into the bucket."

"Like Hansel and Gretel," I say. "She won't get hurt?"

"We'll put a towel in the bottom of the bucket to make it nice and soft and more treats there too. She'll be stuck, but she'll be cozy and safe."

"That's great." It is. It's a smart plan. At the same time, I don't like the idea of my hamster being at the bottom of a bucket all night, all alone.

I take a bunch of our hardcover books off the shelf and stack them to build a staircase. The book-steps go right up to the top of our red cleaning bucket. Mom covers my staircase with a tea towel.

"Now it won't be slippery," she says.

I put another towel at the bottom of the bucket. Then I use the egg and corn to make a trail of treats up the steps and into the bucket. I add a bit of chopped cucumber in case she's thirsty.

"Emi, it's way past your bedtime, and it's school in the morning. Let's head to bed."

I follow Mom down the hallway to our

bedrooms. I give her a big hug goodnight. Once she's closed her bedroom door, I turn around and walk back to the kitchen, slow and quiet, on my tiptoes.

# CHAPTER 14

I lie back down on the kitchen floor by the fridge. My hamster is awake, her black eyes shining. Things feel different at night, quieter. Or noisy in different ways. Back where we used to live, I could hear the frogs croaking at night. In the city, I hear tires splashing in puddles under streetlights, far-off sirens, and the voices of people up late, laughing as they walk down the sidewalk. When it's night, I feel like my sounds have to change too. They have to hush. So when I decide to talk to my hamster, I whisper.

"Hi," I say. "I don't think I've mentioned that I'm Emiko, Emi for short. It's a Japanese name. Emiko means 'illustrious and beautiful girl,' which I am, of course." I do my usual hair flip and fake snob face. I pause. What else can I tell her?

I want her to know that I'm sorry. "I really was hoping to get a dog," I say. "And you're not a dog. I can see that. But that's not your fault." My hamster sits on her haunches. She licks her little pink paws and uses them to brush her ears. She's trying to get clean.

In case she can understand, I keep talking. "You're something different from a dog. Which is not to say you aren't good in your own way. I'm sorry I haven't been a better friend to you."

I try to think of how she is different from a dog. "You don't eat dog food like Hugo does. That's okay. You like nuts." I smile at her. "Actually, I like nuts too."

This gives me a new idea. Very gently, so I don't scare her, I open a cupboard. I take out a bag of trail mix. It's the unsalted kind, the only kind that Mom will buy. For once, that's a good thing. I pick out the peanuts and cup them in my hand like treasure.

I sit back down and push a peanut beside the fridge toward my hamster. "Here," I say.

Her little nose twitches. Then she lowers herself down to all fours and takes a couple of steps forward. I do not even breathe. I do not even think. I just watch. My hamster starts eating the peanut.

Slowly, I lie back down on the floor. I take more peanuts out of my palm. I lay a track of the peanut halves along the floor, from beside the fridge out to where I am lying on my stomach. My hamster crunches on the nuts. I pop one into my mouth and crunch too. She comes closer and closer. Now she starts tucking peanuts into her cheeks for later, like she's packing a suitcase. Her face gets big and lumpy.

My hamster likes peanuts about as much as I do. A lot. For all I know, there are a bunch of things we both like.

She is close enough to grab now, but I don't. I admire her. I put my two palms together to make a bigger cup with my last peanuts in the middle. My hamster sniffs my fingertips with her pretty pink nose. She climbs into my hands. Her feet are warm. "You're a beauty," I say, "and you need a name."

She looks up from the peanut. I lean over and put my nose into her fur. She is dirty and sticky, but she still smells like cuteness and softness and fun.

"What do you think of Mini?" I say. "It's funny because, for a hamster, you are not.

Also, the 'mi' part means 'beautiful,' just like in my name."

My hamster stops chewing and looks straight into my eyes like she couldn't agree more.

"I'll take that as a yes. Also, Mini, you need a bath."

# CHAPTER 15

I carry Mini to the washroom and wonder how to clean a hamster.

"Let's be as careful as possible." When Mom washes something delicate, like her jewellery, she uses a clean toothbrush. We have loads in the bathroom drawer. I pick an orange one—a colour Mom and I do not love—wet it and sit down with Mini in my hand on the bathroom floor. I've shut the door so she can't run away again.

"Here we go, Mini." I stroke her fur lightly with the toothbrush a couple of times. "How's that?"

Mini touches her nose to my thumb, a nudge as if to say, *yes it's fine.*

Mini is a champ. I gently rub her with the

damp toothbrush until all her stickiness is gone. But now she's quite wet.

I pick up the hair dryer. How shall I do this? I choose the lowest setting, hold it as far away from Mini as I can and turn it on. Surprise—Mini loves having her fur blow-dried! (And Mom stays asleep!)

# CHAPTER 16

**W**hile I wait for Soren to let me into our Zoom room, my heart does gymnastics, the kind where you run on a bouncy floor then jump, tuck, roll, flip, run some more, backflip and end up with your feet together and your hands high in the air. My heart does that over and over again. I am showing my family my new friend.

"She is so cool!" says Soren. "So soft!"

"*I* want a mouse!" Mei yells.

"Well, actually, she's a hamster." I hold her against my cheek so Mini can see everyone better and I can feel her warm fur on my face.

# CHAPTER 17

"It is not easy to change. I did not want to leave my home in Comox. I did not want to move away from my aunt and uncle and cousins. But Mom got her dream job. What can you do?"

As I talk to her, I stroke the top of Mini's head.

"And if we had never moved to Vancouver, I would never have discovered bubble tea, which you cannot get in Comox. I would also not have met you, the world's best pocket-sized pet."

Nighttime is magic, Mini and I agree. We chat as we look out at all the city lights. The lights smile back at us like visiting stars.

I tell Mini that she is one of my favourites, beautiful in some of the best ways—gentle, listening and twinkle-eyed.

Mini does not look away when I talk. She looks straight at what I am feeling—sadness, sleepiness, amazement, the relief of having my first city friend and excitement about the ones I'll make next. She sniffs up toward my face. I think she is saying, "Go on. Tell me more."

LIBRARY AND ARCHIVES CANADA CATALOGUING IN PUBLICATION

Title: Emi and Mini / Hanako Masutani ; illustrations by Stéphane Jorisch.
Names: Masutani, Hanako, author. | Jorisch, Stéphane, illustrator.
Identifiers: Canadiana (print) 20230132065 | Canadiana (ebook) 20230132391 | ISBN 9781926890203
(hardcover) | ISBN 9781990598005 (EPUB)
Classification: LCC PS8626.A822 E45 2023 | DDC jC813/.6—dc23

Book design by Elisa Gutiérrez

The text of this book is set in Kopius. Chapter titles are set in YWFT Absent Grotesq.

10  9  8  7  6  5  4  3  2  1

Printed and bound in Canada on ancient-forest-friendly paper.

The publisher thanks the Government of Canada, Canada Council for the Arts and Livres
Canada Books for their financial support. We also thank the Government of the Province of
British Columbia for the financial support we have received through the Book Publishing
Tax Credit program, Creative BC and the British Columbia Arts Council.

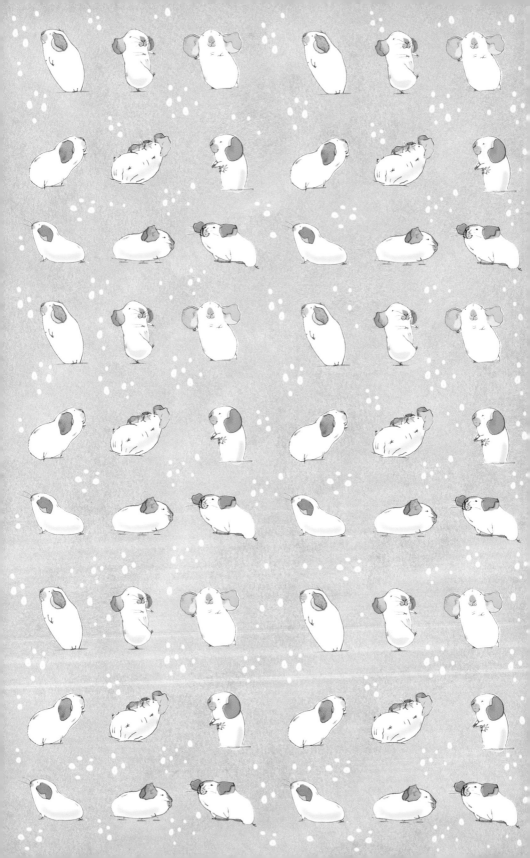

# A New True Book

# MICROSCOPES AND TELESCOPES

**by Fred Wilkin, Ph.D.**

*This "true book" was prepared
under the direction of
Illa Podendorf,
formerly with the Laboratory School,
University of Chicago*

 CHILDRENS PRESS, CHICAGO

Group of objective lenses for a microscope

PHOTO CREDITS

Fred Wilkin—2, 4 (2 photos), 5, 12, 13 (2 photos), 15, 16 (2 photos), 17 (2 photos), 19 (2 photos), 21 (2 photos), 22, 23 (2 photos), 24, 25, (2 photos), 27, 31 (left), 35 (2 photos), 36 (2 photos), 39, 43

Tony Freeman—Cover, 7, 29, 41

Historical Pictures Service, Chicago—9 (2 photos), 10

A. Kerstitch—31 (right), 32, 45 (2 photos)

Library of Congress Cataloging in Publication Data

Wilkin, Fred.
  Microscopes and telescopes.

  (A New true book)
  Includes index.
  Summary: Describes the various parts of a telescope and microscope and their function and discusses the uses of these instruments and how to operate them properly.
  1. Microscopes and microscopy—Juvenile literature. 2. Telescopes—Juvenile literature. [1. Microscopes and microscopy. 2. Telescopes] I. Title.
  QH278.W54  1983      681'.412      83-7592
  ISBN 0-516-01696-2          AACR2

# TABLE OF CONTENTS

Close-up of a microscope and slide.

After examining objects under a microscope, detailed drawings can be made.
Then a model of a bee can be built with scientific accuracy.

# MICROSCOPES AND TELESCOPES

With a microscope you can see small things and make them appear larger. With a telescope you can see faraway things and make them appear larger.

With a telescope you see ships at sea.

Microscopes and telescopes are both kinds of scopes. A scope is an instrument used to see things. One meaning of scope is *to watch* or *to look at.* A scope is used to look at things.

*Micro* means very small. *To look at* + *small things* = a microscope.

Powerful telescopes bring objects at a distance closer.

*Tele* means at a distance.
*To watch + at a distance*
= a telescope.

# EARLY SCOPES

The thing we now call a telescope was once called a looker. Lookers were used for watching battles from a great distance.

It was safe to watch an army from far away, and not be in the middle of the fighting.

In 1608, Hans Lippershey, a maker of eyeglasses, invented the telescope, or looker.

Admiral Nelson (above) used a spyglass, or small telescope. The telescope was invented by a Dutch eyeglass maker named Hans Lippershey (left).

When the Italian scientist Galileo heard about this looker, he decided it could be used for looking at the sky. He would be able to observe the moon and the planets.

Galileo was an Italian astronomer and physicist.

The telescopes that Galileo made and used were simple and not very powerful. However, they helped him and others see things in the sky that had never been seen before.

# EARLY MAGNIFIERS

Long ago, it was seen that clear ball shapes would magnify. Round glass bottles filled with water acted as magnifiers. So did clear rounded shapes of solid glass. To look at small things and make them appear larger, put a clear glass marble on the print on this page.

A bead lens will magnify.

Other early microscopes used a bead of glass much like the shape of a drop of water. Today in some powerful microscopes the lens looks like a tiny bead.

A small beady lens of glass is made using heat.

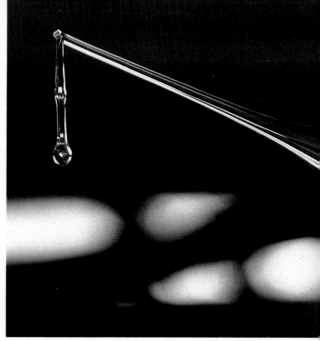

Heat is used to make glass beads.

A thin glass rod is simply
held in a hot flame. It
begins to soften and melt
to form a droplet of glass
that is almost perfectly
round and shiny and clear.
A simple microscope uses
such a glass bead.

# LENSES

A lens is used to focus light. It brings light to a point. Convex lenses are used in most scopes.

There is another type of lens called concave. It appears to be caved in. Concave lenses do not focus light into images. Convex lenses do.

A round glass water bottle can be a lens. It will focus fairly well. Light rays

Can you see
how the bottle
lens magnifies?

pass in through one
curved surface, then
through the water, and out
through a second curved
surface. In and out

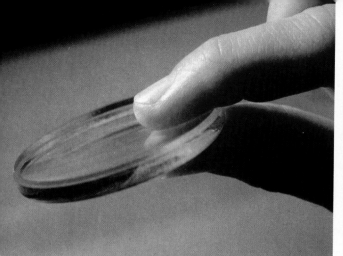

Concave lens (left) and convex lens (right)

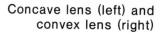

of the surfaces, the light path changes direction.

Light rays passing through a curved clear substance are brought to a point. Looked at sideways, a convex lens is thick in the middle and thinner at the edges.

Concave lens (left) and convex lens (right). Convex lenses (above) come in many sizes and have different curvatures.

Convex lenses can be small or large in diameter. However, there is another difference that is more important. Lenses differ in the curvature of their surfaces. Some are rounded. Some are almost flat, with very little curvature.

# SINGLE LENS
# MICROSCOPES

A single short-focus lens is the main part of this microscope. The lens is supported by a holder that moves. The lens can be adjusted up and down. The knob and a gear move the lens for focusing.

Light from the sun or a lamp shines on the object, or specimen. Light

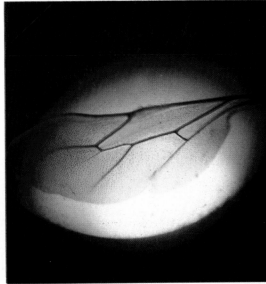

This microscope (left) uses a mirror to reflect more light on a bee specimen. Under a microscope a bee's wing (above) reveals many details not visible to the naked eye.

can also be reflected from below by the mirror to put more light on the specimen.

The microscope keeps things steady and in focus once it is adjusted. You have a free hand for drawing what you see.

With a microscope, you can begin to see the fine details of all kinds of materials and things.

Some kinds of single lens hand microscopes are small. With a glass slide clipped into place and a specimen on it to view,

Pocket microscope (left), a pencil
microscope and salt specimen (right)

this little microscope
provides fifty times
magnification. It is useful
on field trips.

A pencil microscope
does a good job of
magnifying tiny objects like
sand and salt grains when
held close to them.

Simple hand lens

The "scope" of microscopes could include simple hand lenses. Easy to carry and use, they help a keen observer who wants to see many things.

Magnified eyeglass screw (above)
and the workings of a pocket
watch (left)

For example, here is an
eyeglass screw. Have you
seen the inside workings
of a pocket watch?

**23**

Barrel of scope used as lens.

# LENSES AND A TUBE

This is the main part of an old microscope. It is a tube with lenses at both ends. It is bigger than the pencil microscope but works about the same way.

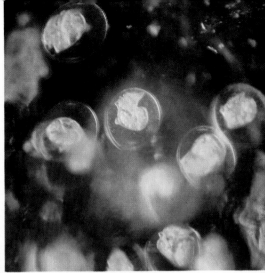

Microscopes can be used
to study marine life,
such as these magnified
snail eggs (above).

The whole tube of this microscope acts like a thick, solid single lens. It can be used and held in this way to examine plant life in an aquarium or for watching a snail. It gives a close-up view of snail eggs.

Usually the tube is fitted into a slider on a heavy base called the foot. Then the tube with its lenses adjusts up and down with a knob and a gear.

The lens called the objective is the one brought close to the slide.

Put a bee wing onto the slide first. Then put the slide on the stage.

The barrel of the scope holds the lenses in position.

Close-up of an objective lens and slide

There are directions and
rules for operating the
microscope. There are
skills to learn. It may be a
sturdy machine, but in
some ways it is delicate.
Use it very carefully.

# ADJUSTING
# A MICROSCOPE

Never turn the adjusting knob so that the barrel moves down while you are looking into the eyepiece.

Instead, look at the slide on the stage from the side. This way you can clearly see the distance between the objective lens and the specimen.

Bring your slide into focus by moving up and away from your slide. Never move the barrel down while you are looking through the eyepiece. If you do, you might smash what you are trying to see.

Get the lens as close as possible to the slide without touching. Then look and get a focus by moving up and away. This saves cleaning or damaging the lens and smashing the slide and whatever is on it.

Some microscopes are built to stop at a limit point. This keeps the objective lens from getting close enough to break anything.

But it is still a good idea to focus while moving the barrel upward. Then, little adjustments can be made to clear up the image.

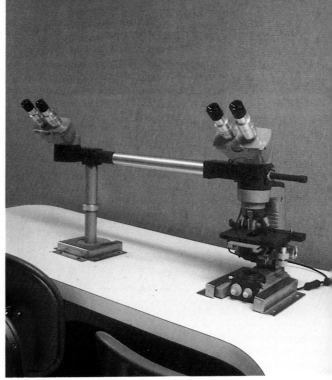

Microscope with its case and lenses (left). With the double microscope (above) a teacher can help the student learn how to use a microscope.

School microscopes are usually sturdy and easy to operate. More detailed microscopes are intended for use by trained scientists.

Solar telescope at Kitt Peak Observatory, near Tucson, Arizona is used to study and photograph the sun.

# TELESCOPE LENSES

In a telescope, the lenses must be combined in a certain way.

A telescope has an objective lens and an eyepiece lens. So does a microscope. How are they different?

The objective lens of a telescope points to an object far away.

The eyepiece lens is for looking through.

The objective lens is convex, but just barely. That means it is only curved slightly. It is just a bit thicker in the middle than at the edges.

The lens has a focus point that is far from the lens.

The eyepiece lens will have a very short focal length.

The two different lenses must be used to look at something far away.

Hold the short one in front of your eye. What you see will be blurry. Move the long focal length lens slowly away until an image comes into view.

Presto, you will see a fairly clear and large "picture" of the faraway scene. Upside down!

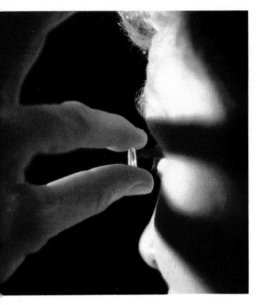

The short focal length lens at the eye (left) is like the eyepiece of a telescope. When paired with a long focal lens (right) you will see faraway objects upside down.

The two lenses will work in combination only at a certain separation.

The tube of a telescope slides a bit in and out, or "telescopes," to adjust for a clear focus.

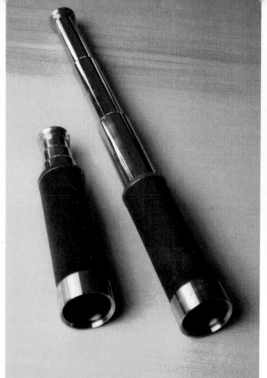

In order to work, telescopes must have a smaller short focal lens and a larger object lens.

# TYPES OF TELESCOPES

The spyglass adds another lens in the eyepiece part that is exactly like the eyepiece lens. It turns the image right side up. Lenses do flip flops.

The spyglass magnifies twenty-five times. That is a fairly good magnification.

Another type of telescope can be mounted on a stand so that it moves very little while you look through it.

This type might have prisms inside that act like mirrors for the path of light through the scope. It keeps the length shorter so it does not need to "telescope" in and out. The light is traveling a much greater distance through the scope than it appears to be.

Another kind of telescope that does not magnify as greatly uses an objective lens, a thin convex lens with a long focal length. But instead of another little convex lens, it uses a concave eyepiece

Binoculars
magnify images
right side up.

lens. This arrangement
gives a right-side-up image.
It is used in binoculars.
This means two oculars or
eyepieces.

Sometimes a monocular
scope has one such lens.

# TELESCOPE MAGNIFICATION

An astronomical refractor-type telescope on a tripod stand may have a set of different eyepieces, depending on whether you want high or low power magnification.

A long-focus objective lens may need ten inches to focus an image. The eyepiece may focus at two

Telescopes are used to study the stars.

inches. Ten divided by two
is five—and that is the
magnification power—5X.

The telescope that
Galileo used was about
6X. It magnified about the
same as binoculars used
for watching birds or
football games.

A telescope's objective lens may be marked 700 millimeters. The eyepiece ocular may be marked 7 millimeters. Seven hundred divided by seven is one hundred, or 100X for that set of lenses. We get higher powers with a shorter focal length eyepiece. Lower powers use a longer focus eyepiece.

Each type of telescope lens will focus light differently.

# REFLECTING TELESCOPES

A round, slightly concave mirror in a telescope reflects light back to a focus. Another mirror can bounce light to one side and out of the tube to an eyepiece lens.

Very large mirrors gather a great deal of light from very faint stars. Focusing on a film, the image can be photographed for study.

The Palomar telescope in California has a 200-inch mirror. It has charted the heavens and discovered many light sources very far away.

Outside view and looking from the inside of the solar telescope at Kitt Peak Observatory near Tucson, Arizona.

# AIDS TO THE EYE

The eye is marvelous, but it has limits. Microscopes and telescopes help us see things our eyes alone never could see.

# WORDS YOU SHOULD KNOW

**binocular**(by • NOCK • yoo • ler) — a device with two eyepieces used to view objects

**command**(kuh • MAND) — to direct; be in charge or control

**concave**(KAHN • kaive) — curved inward

**convex**(KAHN • vex) — curved outward

**curvature**(KER • vah • cher) — to be curved

**focal length**(FOE • kil • LENGTH) — the distance between a lens and where the light waves meet after leaving the lens

**focus**(FOE • kuss) — the point where rays of light meet after being bent by a lens

**image**(IM • ij) — the picture formed by light shining through a lens

**lens**(LENZ) — a piece of clear material that has been shaped to cause light rays that pass through it to meet or spread out

**magnify**(MAG • nih • fye) — to make an object appear larger

**magnifier**(MAG • nih • fire) — an instrument that makes objects appear larger

**microscope**(MIKE • roh • skoap) — an instrument that makes a very small thing look larger

**monocular**(mon • OCK • yoo • ler) — a device with one eyepiece used to view objects

**objective**(ob • JEK • tiv) — the part of the microscope, the lens, that first receives the light rays from the object to be viewed

**ocular**(OCK • yoo • ler) — the eye piece of a microscope

**prism**(PRIH • zim) — a transparent solid object in the shape of a triangle that bends light

**reflect**(re • FLEKT) — to throw back light rays that strike a surface

**refract**(re • FRAKT) — the bending of light rays as they pass through one substance to another

**scope**(SKOAP) — a device that you use to view something

**telescope**(TEL • es • skoap) — a device that makes distant objects appear closer and larger

**tripod**(TRY • pod) — a stand with three legs

# INDEX

*About the author*

*Fred Wilkin, Jr. is the Chairman of Natural Science at National College of Education. He has written scripts and acted as science consultant for a number of films and film strips on natural phenomena for Journal Films and SVE. Dr. Wilkin also has written science investigations for Ginn's science programs for grades 1 through 8.*